One Man's Life...
.... Another Man's Death

A Novel of a Hitman,
Love, Passion, and Steaming Sex

D A N   D I A S I O

ISBN 978-1-63784-408-3 (paperback)
ISBN 978-1-63784-409-0 (digital)

Hawes & Jenkins Publishing
16427 N Scottsdale Road Suite 410
Scottsdale, AZ 85254
www.hawesjenkins.com

Printed in the United States of America

A Time in The Life of a Hitman

DEDICATION AND ACKNOWLDGEMENTS

RIP my friend... Joe
And to my friend Phil

Previous Publications by Dan Diasio

My first book was a self-help book, "In Between Marriages", on single parenting, published by Sully in 1971.

I was twice President and Chapter Parliamentarian of PWP Chapter 160, Sheepshead Bay, Brooklyn, NY. I was also Regional PWP Parliamentarian and gave workshop lectures on, "The Parliamentary Procedure", for running their chapter meetings.

I took what I learned and filled the void created in the subject of handling a divorce and raising a child alone.

My second book was inspired by a worldwide treasure hunt challenge.

A dog, out for a leisurely stroll with his master, suddenly started scratching at the earth as if it was desperately trying to uncover a prized buried bone. The prize that he unearthed was a beautiful precious-stone broach.

This was the culmination to a feverish hunt. Thousands were searching for this prized piece of jewelry that was buried somewhere in the English countryside—not because it was so valuable; not because it was so beautiful; not even because it was finders-keepers—but because it was a challenge.

There is a growing community of these challenge-seeking treasure hunters. Long before Kit Williams wrote his book of clues to the whereabouts of that broach in "Masquerade", there were always those who were drawn by the fascination of buried treasure.

In the days gone by, Spanish Galleons were plundered by pirates of the high seas. Some of the more famous pirates, like that of Captain Kidd, did bury their booty for some later retrieval and mapped the location of its burial site. To insure against losing the treasure, if perhaps the map fell into the wrong hands, they skillfully clouded it with pseudo-locations, underlying descriptions, and verse. Even today, searching for old pirate treasure continues. The most famous of the pirate treasures is said to be buried on Pine Island. The treasure is said to consist of gold and jewels and at the bottom of a pit on this very tiny island. The problem here is that the pit continually fills with water as a well does and never empties itself. Myth has it that seven people will die before the treasure is found. So far, six have fallen to this fate in the search.

Around the turn of the century, a man lying on his deathbed gave clues of his buried millions in the way of three ciphers. Only the first cipher has been decoded correctly (by using the text of the Declaration of Independence) and it purports that the treasure is buried in the Blue Ridge Mountains. Many have claimed to have decoded the other ciphers (all differently) but yet none have claimed the treasure, which is said to be worth by today's standards, around two billion dollars!

Other lost treasures have not yet been found—like that of Solomon's Mines, The Incas Treasure, and the treasure of The Lost Dutchman. All this intrigue and fascination has led to the birth of the modern-day treasure hunt. Kit Williams could lay claim to its birth, but the real author and father of the treasure hunt was born out of its challenge of wit and sleuthery. Contests and games by the hundreds have been devised to feed this challenge. Everyone will admit to themselves quite readily as to their ability, cunning and cleverness toward interpretation.

In an untitled sequel book, where the idea was to discover the hidden title, Kit Williams carefully hid bees among the beautiful pictorial pages. When you correctly selected a page with bees, the number of bees corresponded with that number letter of the alphabet. i.e.-A being 1 and Z being 26. When completed and un-jumbled, you come up with the title, "Bees Only Sing". Kit now added a little twist: you were to submit your answer without using the written word! Now, that might take some thought. I submitted my losing entry by using the pictogram, better known as Hieroglyphics.

Most modern-day treasure hunts offer prizes that are quite modest in comparison to the original pirate treasures. While some offer gold, silver, or jewels valued at from five thousand to around fifty thousand, there was one treasure hunt game, produced by Warner Communications entitled simply. "Treasure", that was worth an additional ten thousand dollars.

Many of these games are solvable by the clues in the book, so the literal outdoors search is unnecessary.

Two Californians, a retired police detective and an assistant DA teamed up to meet this challenge. But alas, their correct solution came two months after the expiration of the contest, when the million-dollar prize had been donated to charity. However, they did get to keep the $10,000 golden horse they unearthed.

The same dynamic duo has traveled the entire country hunting and searching for, "Treasure of the Tarot".

In this book, if you can discover, just from the written clues in a story, a diamond and gold unique pendant & chain worth $25,000 could be yours

$11.95

Buried in the public domain within a thirty-five-mile radius of New York City is a selected Tarot card. As explained in the *Treasure of the Tarot: A Modern Day Treasure Hunt*, this card, when found, is redeemable for a diamond, emerald, and gold pendant worth over $25,000.

If you can interpret the clues correctly, you can discover the exact location to dig or you can simply submit the location on the form included in the book and, if correct, the pendant will be delivered to you!

The pendant itself is based on the design of a Tarot card by Pamela Coleman Smith and was manufactured by Monzón Goldsmith of Keyport, New Jersey.

For all lovers of the Tarot and mystery fans everywhere, *Treasure of the Tarot: A Modern Day Treasure Hunt*, authored by Daniel Diasio and produced by Dandy Enterprises, cannot fail to entice you into this real life treasure hunt.

DANIEL DIASIO met his wife, Yvonne, through the organization Parent's Without Partners, Inc., where they both served on the Board of Directors. They married on Valentine's Day in Sally Jesse Raphael's Wine Press restaurant, with Ms. Raphael as the "best man." The author has been interested in treasure hunt games ever since they were introduced by Kit Williams in his first book, *Masquerade*. His other interests include ancient civilizations, parapsychology, and the outer space connection. He is an artist in oils and pastels, and enjoys collecting antique furniture, as well as coins, stamps, and antique pens.

Vantage Press, Inc.
516 West 34th St., New York, N.Y. 10001

ISBN 0-533-10880-2

9 780533 108800

90000>

My son, Dan, made the investment while I wrote the book and had a professional do the drawings. It was published in 1994 by Vantage Press. The treasure of the tarot was never found before its expiration of 12/31/1999.

My third book is one about my family, "Of Hearts and Dreams", published in 2005 by Media Kindle.

This novel is a combination of fact and fiction about Gabriella, a young single parent, a descendant of Rosina, is enveloped by my real Italian Family...truly a blend of strife, endurance and passion. Her heartwarming home life is contrasted with a battling business life and a challenged love affair with Dax, her suave, handsome, South American boss, who had deep secrets of his own.

My fourth book is my autobiography, "I Led Four Lives... Confessions of a Dead Gangster".

"I Led Four Lives" encompasses the professional me, the artistic me, the playboy me and the gangster me. I will attempt to show how, upon birth, I was predisposed and predestined to live four distinct but simultaneous lives.

If you are old enough you may have heard of the old cold-war television show in the early 50's called, "I led three lives." The three lives plot consisted of a normal 30s-40's middle class man, his life as a Communist, an FBI spy, and Communist counterspy. In that TV series, Herbert Philbrick is played by Richard Carlson and was a very big hit.

Well, I will now tell you my story of, "I Led Four Lives".

It may not be as exciting as being an international "007" spy but my four lives were truly more exciting and dangerous to me, and after reading it you may even agree. I may not have been of the 007 caliber, but maybe a 004 or 005. It's more like I lived the story of the movie released in 2002, "Catch me if you can", starring Tom Hanks and Leonardo DiCaprio. My activities preceded that film by about 40 years.

I'm not proud of some of the stupid choices I have made growing up. What I am proud of is the accomplishments I've done in each of the four lives I've led.

I was tested by Mensa in the early 70's and have a certified Intelligence Quotient of one hundred fifty-one (151). I wonder what I would have accomplished if I devoted myself at a young age to being completely legit? I probably would be rich like my brother, close to ½ Billion dollars. I think I may have made quite the prosecutor if I pursued that line of career.

Actually, I would have been successful in any endeavor I pursued.

Other publications include newsletters and business columns, and…

Lyricist for two off –Broadway musicals, "Rumplestiltskin" and "The Laughing Feather".

I wrote songs for Engelbart Humperdinck, Johnny Paycheck, Herminie Gingold, Steve Lawrence and Edie Gourmet and many other stars.

I wrote lyrics and music and produced three albums and 36 songs across all venues. They were all produced in Nashville, TN, by Paramount Music, featuring the Paramount Band and singers. I also wrote an anthology of works and short stories.

I have over 100 copywriten musical compositions.

Look for my new 5th book soon to be released:

One Man's Life...
Another Man's Death
By Daniel J. Diasio

Novel of A Hitman, Love, Passion, and Steaming Sex

A Time in The Life of a Hitman

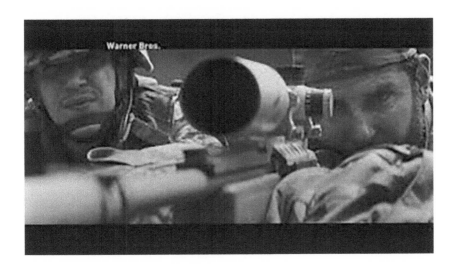

PROLOGUE

I agreed to meet them at 1:00 PM. Making my way through the theater district of Manhattan, I crossed Eighth Avenue and amidst a torrid of advertising signs and entered the Play-Bill Lounge.

Leaving the bustle, din and the bright sun behind, I ventured into the cool darkness. Once inside, I stood for just a moment, letting my eyes get adjusted to the dimly lit interior. Scanning the room with walls covered in red flocked paper and furniture of dark mahogany, I saw that I was the first to arrive.

I walked to the end of the bar and sat on the last stool where the bar rounded itself. I would be facing everyone who entered without being too conspicuous.

I was about ten minutes early so I ordered a scotch and soda. I usually drink scotch on the rocks, but I figured it was still early and I'd better nurse it. I took a cigarette out my pack of Marlboro's and lit it. I was just finishing my first sip when I spotted Jerry coming through the door. He was followed by an older man, and through the still open door could see a burly man in topcoat and hat, taking up his sentry position directly at the entrance.

I stepped off the stool and with drink in one hand and the cigarette in the other, strode to them briskly before they were able to reach the bar.

"Hi, Jer--just got here myself," I said, not offering my hand but instead motioning toward a vacant booth in the back, away from the bar with its three patrons. I slid in on one side and they both slid in opposite me, first the older man and then Jerry.

Jerry introduced the short, slim, balding, elegantly dressed man, who appeared to be about forty, as Joe. No last name--just Joe. It wouldn't be till much later in our business relationship that I discovered that this man was Joe Colombo, Capo of one of New York's five crime families; his terf being the territory of Bensonhurst, Brooklyn.

At the time of that meeting, I knew all too well of the Mafia or Cosa Nostra. It was our thing. I knew all about the crime families that everyone sees on TV and read about in the papers. I was involved with the Bronx family and had never met Joe before. When I first got involved with Jerry Tartakow, I was a foolish, young photographer with a passion for love and adventure.

At twenty years old I had just got married, was very naive' and didn't have a clue to what I was getting myself involved in.

For me it was to be the beginning, the beginning of a long but steady climb within the Mafia's crime organization; the world's largest controlled syndicate, profiting more than any other conglomerate serving the public--and the Mafia does serve the public! In its own right, a very well-run, well-policed government.

I rose through the family, learning quickly--but sometimes the hard way-- reaching the niche where I find myself today; Joe Colombo's top bodyguard and one of the organization's top cleaners--a hit man--a button man. Whatever you want to call it, it still comes out the same--a murderer for the mob!

Yes--a hired killer just like Paladin on that old TV show, with his "Have Gun--Will Travel" card--except without the card. It's strictly business. A service for the mob.

I guess I think of it like...like I'm a cop. In society's regular world, when somebody breaks the law, a cop makes the arrest, a jury tries him, and a court judge sentences him. Well, the Mafia has its own social structure and discipline too. When we have a problem, we have to deal with it ourselves. We take care of our own. The Capo, or boss, is the judge and jury. I'm the policeman and executioner. Most of the time I don't even know who the targets are or what they did wrong--and it doesn't matter--not to me. I mean it's not as if I don't have a conscience or have feelings. These guys I hit knew the chance they were taking when they broke the sacred oath, the one they swore to uphold...in blood. There are only four reasons a guy gets hit. One-he steals; two--he fools around with another made guy's girl; three--he kills without sanctioning; and four--he is too power hungry.

So, you see, that's why they call me the cleaner--I clean up their messes. It's a police action by a society accepted by its people. A service job and strictly business!

CHAPTER ONE

Chucka opened his eyes. They felt heavy and his vision blurred. He strained and tried to clear them. Gradually they had begun to focus, and he started to search for recognizable objects in this drab, pale-yellow room in which he found himself.

And then it hit him. A deep dull ache in his right side. He couldn't move--he could barely try. The antiseptic smell filtered through his nostrils and settled in his head, biting at his brain.

"Ea--Chucka. Chucka, it's me, Joey. Just lie still and don't try to talk. Doc says you're gonna make it."

Joe leaned closer to Chucka and glanced at his bodyguards standing by the door. "Don't worry 'bout nothin'. I'm gonna take care of this now. I just want to say thanks. You're a good man."

Joe sat on the edge of the bed, as if to pause a moment before continuing. "You were hit pretty bad, but the Doc did a fine patch-up job. You took one in da arm and one in da side. That bastard was never very good with heat even when he was wit' me. You took him out before he was able to finish you off and get to me." Then it all flashed back in Chucka's mind.

He was just coming out of DaVinci Pizzeria on 18th Avenue in Brooklyn, around 65th street, when it happened. Joe was still inside, just behind Chucka. For a second there was a tremendous burning sensation, before Chucka went into shock.

He drifted into a kind of limbo state--everything moving in sort of slow motion. He felt a second impact but this time there was no pain. He didn't know what he was doing as his reflexes took over and he went on automatic. The only thing he knew was he had a gun in his hand, and he was using it. Chucka saw the guy going down at the same time his own legs crumbled and gave way.

CHAPTER TWO

It was Friday night's poker at Junior's Pork Store. He had the perfect back room, protection from all sides. Junior was Joe Columbo's cousin and hosted the weekly game. The game consisted of about seven, sometimes eight players, if you include Joe Colombo Sr. He only played about twice a month. Other weekly players included: Joe Jr., Anthony, Caesar, Chucka, Duckfeet, Cousin Junior and Jerry Cadillac.

It was right out of an episode of the TV show, "Soprano's". There was always free hot food, freshly cooked by Cousin Junior's wife Carmela. There has been business aplenty, fun galore, and usually a winning night for Chucka.

Guys in the game ran cigarettes and guns from South Carolina. They were the first to do that. The whole crew sold them right out of the trunks of their own cars for $1.25 a carton. That was in 1961.

It was the following night that Chucka found himself sitting at a table in a small neighborhood Italian Restaurant on Nostrand Avenue in Brooklyn called Piccolo Pino's. He had been invited to a meeting by representatives of 'Crazy Joey Gallo'. I think he got that nickname because he had a violent temper and kept a lion as a pet.

There was always bad blood between Gallo and Colombo ever since Persico died. Joe had tried to make peace by asking for a meeting and offered a $1,000 bill. Gallo was offended and refused the meeting proposal.

So, it came to head with the two Joes. Now, with Joe Colombo getting notoriety with his Italian American Civil Rights League and the march on the F.B.I. headquarters...well, that didn't sit right with the Gallo brothers or Carlo Gambino, so the "Don" gave his sanctioning--Colombo was to be hit!

But the difficulty is in getting to a Capo. He is always surrounded by his henchmen entourage and bodyguards--and Chucka was his personal bodyguard. To get to Colombo they had to, either figuratively or literally, go through Chucka--the choice would be his.

An offer was made and Chucka said no thank you, "Maybe some guys don't, but I believe in keeping loyal to the man who helps you earn".

Chucka would have been killed right on spot, if it weren't for the gun he had in his hand. Whenever Chucka went to a meeting on business he always wore a pair of pants with the pocket cut out so he could reach the gun he had strapped to the inside of his leg. No guy was going to check him there. That was the only way he could have pulled it off. They weren't about to let him go to the toilet and come out blasting with a previously concealed gun. Hell, everybody saw that in "The Godfather".

After Chucka said 'no', one of the two buffers, the tall skinny one with part of his left ear missing, broke the sudden silence, "I'm really sorry to hear you say that", he exclaimed with a cruel grin.

Chucka took his hand from his pocket and laid the gun on the table, leaned slightly forward, and asked, "Now, why is that?" in his best cocky-bluff-posture he could muster under the given conditions.

"We'll be seeing you!" the same Gallo representative said in a low steady intense tone that left nothing to be questioned as to his meaning. He got up and left with his two cohorts in crime.

By saying no, it made him a target. He thought he could handle it. He couldn't. Chucka made one mistake--he didn't tell Colombo. And it almost cost him his life.

CHAPTER THREE

T he door to the hospital room opened and in walked a nurse announcing, "You'll have to leave now Mr. Colombo. He lost a lot of blood and is still very weak. He needs all his rest--Doctor's orders."

Joe walked to the side of the bed where Chucka could best see him. He leaned over Chucka and looked at him with concerned eyes,

"Thanks kid. I won't forget this. And don't worry, Sheila and the kids are safe and well cared for. They're throwin' me outa' here now, but I'll see you soon. Just you concentrate on getting better. Chow."

As Joe turned to leave, Chucka closed his eyes and in a brief second heard the door close behind them. He was tired and drained of all energy.

Fragments of his life began to pass in front of him, as if his eyelids were a screen. His mind drifted and he saw himself when he was twenty-one, the time it all began. It was early dawn and on this particular Saturday in June of '62. The Henry Hudson Parkway looked especially pretty this time of year. Chucka thought the area just around the Cloisters overlooking the Hudson River was most serene and scenic. He loved stopping there on his way to the Bronx just to relax for a brief moment and enjoy the freshness in the air.

He was going to enjoy today. He liked shooting weddings, they are always festive--that's their nature. He was to shoot the color slides and Cookie, a pretty young thing, was to shoot the black & whites for the albums. He was glad Cookie worked for the same studio he did. He liked working with her--she was a good photographer--and he thought they made a good couple.

Back on the roadway now, he thought of how much he had missed Cookie. He thought of her pert 5'2" body, well shaped for its size. He thought of her long black hair cascading past her shoulders, stopping just short of her luscious round ass. He thought of a fantasy he would like to act out with her. He thought of her being his...permanently.

Chucka drove along Castle Hill Avenue as he has done many times before; to swing by the studio in order to pick up Cookie and the photo equipment before going to the bride's house to start work. He couldn't get her off his mind--not that he really wanted too. His mind fumbled through thoughts of sex and times of intimacy he had spent with Cookie--just one week earlier.

They had a date that started out at Giuseppe's Italian Restaurant Just off of Brighten Beach Avenue and Serf Avenue. They had great food there and he was able to get his favorite dishes, stuffed artichoke, and broccoli rabe & hot sausage.

After desert of Tiramisu and Italian coffee with anisette, Chucka paid the check, intentionally leaving a generous 35% tip. He respected people who worked for tips to make a living. It also made him look beneficial in nature and not just a hood.

When they stepped out in the September brisk air, they hugged. He put his arm around her shoulder holding her close as they walk toward the amusement park. They went on a few wild rides including the, 'Tilt-a-whirl', roller coaster, 'Thunderbolt', 'The Tunnel of Love', and the 'House of Horrors'.

They settled down on his jacket he laid on the beach. They cozied up to each other under this half-moon illumination.

They kissed passionately while fondling each other's body. They spent the good part of an hour there before driving home.

Forward a week, as he approached the photography studio, he anticipated the day's events and possibly the evening ones if what he had in mind for Cookie worked out. He could feel the stirring beneath the fly of his pants.

He swung out of the driving lane and pulled up to the curb in front of the "Shutter-Bug Portrait and Wedding Photographers Studio."

With great anticipation and wearing an equally big smile, he strode confidently to the door, took a deep breath, and opened it. He stepped into the waiting room, adorned with all sorts of framed portraits of babies in cute poses and various brides in gowned splendor.

Instead of finding himself in the presence of one fine chic called Cookie, he came face to face with a man in his mid-thirties and slightly over six feet tall.

"You must be Chucka," he said, as more of a statement than a question.

Chucka nodded without saying a word. "I'm Jerry, Cookie's brother. Cookie called me last night and asked me to fill in for her today. She got the flu," he cordially said while extending his hand for an acquaintance handshake.

Chucka, trying not to display any disappointment, accepted the greeting and said,

"I'm sorry to hear she's not felling too well--hope she gets better soon."

"She'll be okay in a few days. She just picked up a little bug," Jerry explained.

"So, you're Cookie's brother. She's told me a lot about her only brother. She rates you high and says you're a good photog too," Chucka mused,

"Well, you know how kid sisters can be,".

Jerry chuckled, "Sometimes a little over-boasting and at other times they are in complete denial that you exist."

Chucka grinned and nodded even though he really didn't know--not having a kid sister of his own. He often wished he had a sister. Being the youngest of six boys in his family, he didn't have anyone he could confide in. He couldn't talk to his brothers. There was just too much of an age gap between them, Chucka being a change of life baby. They seemed to him to be in a different generation. Besides, there were just some things you couldn't tell another guy!

Chucka's Mom died when he was nine, so there wasn't much of that feminine softness and understanding around him. When she was alive, she was always just too busy, and it seemed to him there was never any time he could just sit down and talk to her.

So now, here was Chucka, forced to work with this man he had just met, instead of spending what he anticipated to be a very enjoyable day--and possibly evening-- with Cookie. Jerry had no way of knowing what Chucka had in mind for his sharp chic of a sister.

Chucka took a deep breath and exhaled slowly, saying to himself, "I just ain't got no fuckin' luck. Guess I gotta just keep Peter in his pants. Damn cunt! She would have to go and get sick! Yeah--sick! Hell, she probably got laid too much last night. Damned bitch!", he thought, but really didn't mean it. It was mere frustration and disappointment. He would miss her.

"Want some coffee?", Jerry asked.

"Huh? Oh--yeah, sure," Chucka answered as reality rudely crashed his daydreaming.

Chucka accepted the cup being handed him and muttered, "We better get started soon."

He briefed Jerry on the day's assignment. Downing the last of the container in one gulp, Chucka asked, "Ready?"

"Yeah."

"Okay, we're outta here." Jerry picked up the equipment case marked 'Cookie' and said, "My car or yours?"

"Let's take yours," Chucka answered, "I'm tired of driving. Takes me an hour to get here from Brooklyn--if there's no traffic and no construction. That's where I hail from--now anyhow." Chucka grabbed a spare strobe and followed Jerry out, letting the front door close behind him a little quicker than he was ready for. It was all he could do to keep his balance and not fall to the pavement. It looked like a routine. Right out of one of those old slapstick comedy movies. Chucka was grateful the din of the avenue covered his predicament and Jerry never noticed a thing.

CHAPTER FOUR

Parked at the curb was Jerry's late model Cadillac. A beautiful white El Dorado.

"Nice, very nice," Chucka offered while sliding into the plush front seat next to Jerry.

"Thanks. I like fine things; a fine car, a fine home, and fine women," Jerry boastingly replied.

"Sounds good to me," Chucka laughed as he noticed that Jerry mentioned women in the plural sense, and wondered if he fooled around. He knew Jerry was married--Cookie told him so.

Chucka fumbled with a pack of cigarettes and offered one to Jerry. He studied Jerry's face for that brief moment, not wanting to stare--or even worse, getting caught starring and having Jerry think he was gay! He had a handsome face, not an ounce of extra fat, and with good classic features. His hair grayed distinguishingly at the temples and had a smattering of gray strands throughout his otherwise thick, black hair. He was dressed in what appeared to be a very expensive suit, styled in the smartest of fashions.

"Maybe he is a pussy man," Chucka thought to himself, "and today might not be such a disaster after all."

Chucka liked weddings and todays wouldn't be any differ-ent. He'd be out there working the wedding and the females. He'd start out by surveying the selection and then move in with a routine that never fails. That's right never fails. Because of the congenial, happy atmosphere and the addition of an abundance of alcohol at most weddings, it was very easy to pick up a girl, even a married one! With not too much effort, Chucka mused, one could make out very well at the wedding reception, maybe even better than the groom--and he knows where he'll be dip-ping it that night.

You play on their vanity…and all women are vain. Women loved to be photographed. Maybe it's that hidden secret desire of all women, at one time or another in their lives, to be a model. Maybe it's the image of themselves that they see as being sexu-ally alluring and desirable. Whatever the reason, they all like it.

Even if they protest and say no--that they don't think they look good in photographs, they all still crave the attention that being photographed brings. Chucka made it more than once with a broad because of a little camera attention.

As they drove toward the bride's house, Chucka's mind drifted to a time about a year earlier.

He was on a wedding assignment by himself one particular Saturday morning and was at the bride-to-be's home. He was busy taking the traditional pictures of her in her bedroom as she prepared for the big event in her life.

Chucka arranged her 3/4 length gown in a circular fashion as she sat in the middle of her bed. She held her bouquet at her waist just under her ponderous breasts. He had to admit that the way the flowers framed those swelling orbs made them appear more predominant and was certainly an eye-catching sight. It put a little throb in his heart as well as one in his pants.

He focused his camera and asked her to wet her lips.

Her rich full lips parted slightly, and a seductive tongue moistened them in such a manner he thought there might be a second meaning. Chucka shook it off as just his own horniness acting up and settled back to the business at hand.

After that pose he took her flowers and set them aside. Taking her extended hand, he helped her off the bed.

She rose, standing close to Chucka. Smiling sweetly and with eyes wide, she asked, "Like to kiss the bride good luck?"

Without waiting for an answer, she closed her eyes and leaned forward, hard against Chucka's surprised body.

With his hands on her shoulders, he kissed her softly.

She opened her eyes and with a pout of a sad child exclaimed, "Boy! If that kiss represents the amount of luck, you wish me, I guess you don't want me to be very happy."

With more fear than embarrassment, Chucka pulled her in close. There was no doubt that she could feel the heaviness at his groin. He kissed her deeply, searching out her tongue with his.

He didn't know whether she was just a cockteaser and would scream at any moment or not. Chucka was determined to find out.

He dropped his right hand from her shoulder and passed it over the top of her protruding breast. She breathed deep at his touch, and he molded her breast as if it were rising dough, then searched out its nubile tip.

She responded with a hand to his inner thigh. In one quick movement she was rubbing the length of Chucka's manhood. They were still kissing.

Chucka sucked at her tongue as it worked around his. She sucked on his as if it were a mini penis.

Without breaking their kiss, her fingers found the zipper to his fly and was soon inside prying free the length of this hot, corralled stallion. She pressed her palm against the acorn shaped head and felt its heat. Encircling the staff below its head, she squeezed. She slowly slid her hand down to its base of thick hair where she first cupped and then massaged his aching testicles.

Chucka broke the kiss and gasped for air. Breathing heavily, he looked into her eyes.

She sensed his urgent need and without saying a word sank to her knees like a mare in heat.

Chucka's large manhood was only a couple of inches from her face, and she couldn't help staring at it. Chucka brought his hands to the back of her head and guided her down until her face was almost touching the giant shaft.

Her lips hovered over it now. She could detect the faint smell of it and thought that she could see a throbbing at the base of its head.

Slowly she reached out her right hand, bringing her fingers first gently in touch with the hot shaft, then wrapping her fingers around its hardness.

She almost gasped at the feel of the giant steel rod in her comparatively small hand. She could feel the desire of it as a pulsating pressure against her slim fingers.

She continued to look at the large organ. Her lips were only about an inch from the head of it.

Chucka could feel the welling up from deep within himself and didn't know how much longer he could contain himself. His hands pressed at the back of her head, urging her lips down to meet the bulbous head of his pride.

Her tongue licked out and pressed against the smooth surface of his shaft.

Chucka's hands tightened on her head. She parted her lips and pressed them in a wet kiss against the head of his manhood. Then she ran her tongue down the hard, blood-engorged shaft.

Chucka let out a strange moaning sound that started deep in his throat and traveled up slowly until it escaped from his gasping mouth, "oh…that feels so good…Oh! Oh!

She took the head of Chucka's pride into her mouth. Her tongue pressed and circled it. She felt the smoothness of it on her lips and against her tongue. Then she gripped the penis by its base and thrust her mouth down on it, taking almost it's full length between her lips.

"Oh, shit," Chucka said involuntarily. His body shuddered at the wonderous sensation of her lips on him. He pressed himself further into her mouth as he thought, "Why do women think deep throating a guy is the end-all for him? But that is not true. The most erogenous zone that gives the most pleasure are the nerve receptors around the base of the head of the penis, not along the shaft, although there are nerves there too, of course."

Her hand started moving rhythmically up and down the hard shaft that protruded from her mouth.

Chucka felt the head of his penis press against the back of her throat. He knew he couldn't hold back much longer. It was heaven.

Her hand continued its pumping action as her mouth sucked on the head and shaft of his swelling organ.

Her head bobbed up and down in frantic motion. Her tongue licked around the glans in her mouth. Her long fingers cupped Chucka's testicles and pressed the tender, sensitive spot between them. Her cheeks puckered as she sucked on the smoothe bulb-like head in her mouth. Her fingers moved faster and faster on his flesh. Her tongue licked at the mass of quivering nerves between her lips. Her teeth nipped at it. Her free hand pressed hiss balls, tickled them, and stimulated the sensitive area around them.

Chucka moaned. He started more actively thrusting his penis into her mouth. His need was more urgent now. His own rhythm sped up as she nipped and sucked at his large organ until she knew he was ready to cum.

Chucka was caught in a most violent of orgasms. It seemed that the spasms would never end--not that he wanted them to. Wave after wave of cream-like sperm shot deep into her throat. She swallowed immediately, not wanting any of his joy juice to spill on her gown.

She liked the taste of it between her lips. She liked sucking on him, it felt overly large and swollen in her mouth. Yet, she had found that she liked its size. It had an intriguing quality of its own.

CHAPTER FIVE

C hucka smiled to himself at these events of a year ago. It was the first time he ever made it with the bride-- before the wedding, anyhow. He was really taken by surprise by it all, but he shouldn't have been. He should have known better than to be surprised about anything when there's a woman involved. They're so unpredictable.

"Chucka--hey Chucka--you with me?" Jerry questioned.

"Oh, ah-yeah. Guess my mind was elsewhere for a moment. What was it you said?"

"I asked you how you got that name, Chucka. It's kind of an odd nickname", Jerry said.

"Oh, that," Chucka half-laughed, "my name is really Phil Rosini, but when I was a kid in school, they called me Chucka because I was tall and played a lot of basketball and got a lot of chucks.

"They weren't going to call me Chuck, which is another boy name. so, they added an 'A' to it and made it Chucka. I wasn't too bad either. I was taller than most kids my age, Well, anyhow, the name stuck."

Jerry pulled the car into a semi-circled driveway and parked in front of a large expensive-looking Tutor-style house.

"Looks like the bride's ol' man got dough," Jerry said as he stepped out of the car. "Where's the reception being held?"

"Over at the Pelham Bay Yacht Club," Chucka answered knowingly. "Could be a lot of rich broads there."

Jerry smiled. This was starting to look better. "Worth looking into," he volunteered as they walked up the five stairs to the front door.

Before Chucka could reach the bell, the door opened and a young man who appeared to be a delivery boy stepped out calling behind himself to a beautiful girl standing just a few feet into the foyer, "Be right back with the rest of the flowers, Miss."

This vision of loveliness, obviously one of the bridesmaids, looked at them both, Jerry first, then Chucka.

With an approving smile, she greeted them, "Hi, I'm Janice. Dotti's my sister."

"Dottie?" quizzed Chucka.

Stepping aside, letting both enter, Janice replied, "Yes, Dorothy Stanton. The bride--remember?"

"Yeah. Ah--thank you miss." Chucka said, feeling a bit foolish at her putdown.

"No need to be formal here", she said, "we're not snobs. Please call me Jan. Come, I'll show you the way."

Simultaneously, Jerry and Chucka looked at each other. Jerry shrugged his shoulders and followed the girl, staring all the while at her well-rounded firm ass. Chucka followed close behind, taking notice of what Jerry was already ogling.

"Dottie's in her bedroom waiting for you." She stopped at the doorway to the bedroom, "she's ready," Janice said, stopped and turned sideways and motioned for them to enter.

Jerry had to turn sideways also, to get through the doorway.

As Chucka entered, Jan extended her left arm across the doorway, blocking his entry and forcing him to abruptly stop in front of her and very close.

Wearing her sexiest and most devilish of smile, she parted her lips and breathed, "Save a couple of shots for me."

Leaning slightly forward and feeling very brave following her obvious advance, whispered from deep in his throat, "I'll always have a hot shot for you, Baby."

She grinned and let him through. Chucka and Jerry quickly got down to business, setting up their cameras and strobe lights.

Chucka saw the way Jerry was working and knew that Cookie was right. Jerry was a pro.

As beautiful as Janice was, she paled in comparison to her sister Dorothy. Chucka silently remarked how she should be in the centerfold of Playboy.

The rest of the morning went routinely and uneventfully, except for a bridesmaid that fainted in church. It wasn't Janice.

They worked together methodically, and not before too long had all the staged shots that they required.

CHAPTER SIX

"I'm proud to introduce, for the first time, Mr. Mrs. Louis and Dorothy DeSantis," the master of ceremonies voice bellowed through the microphone.

Applause filled the air and music from the band echoed loudly.

Flash after flash came from the strobes of Chucka and Jerry as the bride and groom entered the reception hall arm-in-arm.

Glasses were raised as the best man proposed a toast, "I'd like to wish my brother and his new bride a long and healthful life together."

The clinking of spoons on glasses could be heard throughout the room in keeping with the tradition of asking the newlyweds to kiss. Blushing, the couple rose and proceeded to kiss which in turn evoked another reign of applause.

All were now seated, with the band still playing happy tunes, in anticipation of the meal which was to begin.

Beer flowed abundantly and everybody indulged themselves with the bottles of scotch and rye with set-ups already at each table.

There was a traveling bar and an open bar in the rear corner of the room for those who wished for more exotic drinks. As the afternoon progressed, so did the volume of alcohol consumed.

The laughter and noise level grew more intense, and couples overcrowded the dance floor, bumping each other in time with the music.

It was truly a joyous affair.

Normally, Chucka would have staged all the necessary photos earlier; the cutting and feeding of the cake, the throwing of the bouquet, the taking off and throwing of the garter, the putting of the garter by the one guy who caught it, onto the leg and thigh of the gal who caught the bouquet, and so on and on and on. But Jerry and Chucka decided to take advantage of the invitation by the bride and groom, for them to stay for the meal. They would let the wedding's events unfold naturally and capture them candidly.

After a time when most of the shots were in the can, Chucka and Jerry retired to the bar in the alcove in the rear corner of the room. They sat and swapped small talk for a while and surveyed the many pretty women.

"Look at that blonde in the black dress over there," Jerry said, gesturing toward the svelte woman with long hair on the dance floor. "What a piece of ass!"

"Looks good enough to eat," Chucka volunteered. "And my chubby is telling me it agrees."

"Hey, go for it," Jerry prompted. "Don't worry. I won't say anything to Cookie."

"To tell you the truth, she looks like too much of a hassle. Too much work for just a quickie, which is all I would want from her," Chucka explained. "If I'm going to get involved, I'd rather it be with your sister."

"Very noble of you, Chucka, but I guess I have a different outlook,"

Jerry said seriously. "I love women--all women. Maybe I am being ruled by the wrong head, but who cares. Who am I hurtin'? Nobody. They want to get laid just as much as we do, maybe more. So, why not?"

"But what if you're in love with someone--don't you feel guilty or something?", Chucka quizzed.

Jerry turned toward Chucka and before answering lit a Benson & Hedges cigarette. He took a long drag and delayed long enough to think of the right thing to say. "Well, Chucka, if you really want to know, I'll tell you. No, I don't feel guilty," he continued, "not because I don't have a conscience, but because I can separate the two--love and sex.

"Let me explain something to you." Chucka was literally in awe. This older, more experienced man was going to let him in on the secrets of life and of men. He wouldn't miss a word as his attention was riveted on what Jerry was about to say.

"I'm not trying to brag or anything, but you did ask me the question," Jerry said. "In my lifetime so far, I have gone to bed with about two to three hundred different women. And I enjoyed all of them. Of course, some better than others, but that doesn't matter. What I'm getting at is, how can you get the best of the crop if you're dating lots of women, when that special one comes along, she'll stand out among all the others. Besides, by dating a lot, you stand a much better chance of meeting that special one." Jerry took another deep drag on his cigarette before continuing on.

"As far as love versus sex. I have learned to separate the two. Sex is with someone you have not developed a relationship with as yet. It is more lust than anything else. In itself, it can be very rewarding and pleasurable although love is all of that and more. Love is pleasure derived from all five senses: sight, sound, smell, taste and touch. That and how she is with me. Sex is fulfillment of the libido. "Jerry pontificated in a matter-of-fact fashion which led to his sincerity."

"But once you love someone, how can you screw around with anybody else?" asked Chucka, curiously.

"That's a little more difficult to answer," Jerry said with a hint of a little chuckle in his voice.

Jerry readjusted his posture before continuing, "I believe you can love more than one woman at the same time. Each has her own quality. Each can bring you pleasure and happiness in a different way from the others. One may have a great sense of humor, another may be a great athletic competitor, and yet a third may stimulate you mentally. Each could be equally beautiful and sexually equal in bed. Each makes you happy. You love each for their own unique quality."

Jerry downed the last of the liquid in his glass and ordered another drink.

"Don't get me wrong, this may not be for everyone. This is for me. I can't condemn nor condone it. It just suits me--for my way of life", Chucka sat in quiet admiration of this man he had just met. You had to admire anybody who could pull that off!

To continue the conversation, but in a different vein, he asked, "What do you do for a living, Jer?"

"Well, for most of my life I've been in photography, in one form or another. Right now, I'm in the midst of putting together a business. I just got tired of working for somebody else and making them all the money. I bust my ass and all I get is a salary--not even a thank you. The way I figure it, as long as I'm going to bust my ass, it might as well be for myself. That's why I decided to go into business; a business that can make me a lot of cash with the least of risk." Jerry explained.

"Is it in photography?", questioned Chucka.

Jerry didn't answer for a second, but turned, ordered another drink, then asked, "Want another drink, Chucka?"

"Okay."

Turning to the barkeep, Jerry ordered, "Make that two more."

Jerry took a sip from his fresh drink, then, turning back to Chucka said, "Yeah, it's in photography--a movie processing lab. You see, I can get all the business I can handle. It's guaranteed." Jerry frowned a bit, then continued, "but I got one problem. I need one more partner, a working partner. I have one partner now--the guy who will get me all the work. But I need one more, someone to run the business."

"Well, wouldn't you run it?", Chucka questioned.

"No, I couldn't," Jerry said, "I have a record. I got into trouble when I was younger--nothing too serious--but that prevents me from owning a business in my name. I'd be puttin' in almost all the cash."

"Here comes that broad, Jan," motioned Jerry. "Looks like she got the hots for you, Chucka. Hey, go for the gusto. All you got to lose is some pent up frustration. I can finish up here and take the equipment back to the studio."

"Sounds good to me. I could use a good piece right now. Then again, I guess anytime is a good time," Chucka grinned.

"So, this is where you two have been hiding," Jan slurred, just ever so slightly. She was feeling really good and a little high from the consumption of alcohol and the shared joint with the best man.

"Aren't you going to ask me to dance?", proposing her question to Chucka.

The band had just finished a fast dance and Chucka froze at the thought of having to do that. He was a lover, not a dancer, he thought. Even though he knew the steps, he wasn't drunk enough to do them in public. In an instant the panic vanished when he heard them starting a slow tune.

Chucka got off his stool and without saying a word, pulled her to him and danced her to the main floor.

"You married?", he asked.

"No, but something tells me it wouldn't matter to you if I were," Janice chided in a very sexy voice.

"You're right, it wouldn't," Chucka said, as he pulled her in even closer, their bodies now molded to one another.

She could feel him. His every move evoking shudders within her.

The dance floor was crowded with each couple bumping into another.

He couldn't concentrate on her, his mind wandering to thoughts of Jerry's business.

"Let's get outa' here. It's too crowded and noisy. We can go some place for a drink where it's quieter, okay?" Chucka asked.

"Thought you'd never ask," Jan laughed, "but I have my car."

"That's good," he said, "I was counting on it. I don't have mine."

"Let me say good-bye to Sis and I'll meet you out front."

"Okay. Give me five minutes. I have to talk to Jerry" Chucka said, before turning and walking back to the bar.

CHAPTER SEVEN

J erry had carefully planted the idea of going into business
into Chucka's mind--and it worked. Chucka would like his
own business. Even more, make a lot of money.

"Hey, Jerry," Chucka said, "ya know…I've been thinkin'
'bout what you said, 'bout your business, I mean. Why couldn't
I be your partner?

I always wanted my own place and I agree with your
thoughts 'bout makin' money."

"Well, I don't know," Jerry replied. "The guy I'm looking
for has to be sharp, somewhat of an actor, not afraid to take
chances and have about two grand to invest. The right man will
earn between five hundred and a thousand a week, so for that
kind of dough he's got to be good. Do you think you can fill the
bill?" Not waiting for an answer, Jerry continued. "Before you
answer, I want you to think about it over the weekend and I'll
do the same. Even if you say yes, there's alot of questions that
need to be answered before I can decide. Give me your number
and I'll call you on Monday morning. If by then you want to
look into it further, we can all sit down and go over the details."

"That sounds fair to me," Chucka replied, as he began to write his phone number on the inside of a matchbook that lay on the bar.

"By the way," Jerry inquired, "what happened with the chic?"

"We're gonna leave now. I'm gotta meet her out front."

Chucka handed Jerry the matchbook, "Here's my number. Guess I'll hear from you on Monday. I'll be home all mornin'."

"Right--and have a good time," Jerry said while motioning toward the outside with his head.

"That's the plan." Chucka turned toward the exit.

Once outside, Chucka stopped, took a Marlboro from his vest pocket pack, put it to his lips and lit it between cupped hands to prevent the wind from blowing out the flame.

"Over here," Janice called from behind the wheel of her fire-engine-red Pontiac GTO.

Chucka slid in next to her. He swung his left arm over her shoulder.

"Hey, you sure move fast. I don't even know your name," she said, feigning annoyance.

"I'm Chucka to my friends. Non-friends can kiss my ass," he cracked.

"You're being too kind to non-friends, Chucka--whatever a Chucka is., "she flashed back.

"You're a real smart-ass, aren't you?", Chucka complained.

She leaned toward him, "I'm sorry. I would like to get to know you better." As Janice was saying this her hand strayed over his lap and her probing fingers were feeling for his quickly responding manhood.

"You just keep- on doing what you're doing and I'll cum in my pants. So stop where you are Jan, or we'll be wasting a hot shot.," Chucka choked.

27

"Perish forbid that should happen in my new car, Chucka," she murmured as she leaned full against him, pressing her two, full breasts hard against him as she kissed him full on the mouth.

Chucka breathed hard as her tongue moved in and out of his mouth, causing him to almost burst in orgasm with the swelling and throbbing of his penis.

His hand was under her gown now, his index finger rubbing against her panties, outlining her luscious mound.

"Hey, baby, let's do somthin' 'bout this," Chucka panted, "I don't like getting laid in a car."

"Okay, let's go to my place. I'd like to change out of this gown, and we can be more comfortable. Besides," she added, "I gotta use the john."

Jan swung the GTO out of the parking lot and headed it toward her apartment.

About ten minutes later she pulled her car into the garage under her building and parked it in her appointed space. Hugging each other, they took the elevator to the third floor.

Janice opened the door to apartment 3C and turned on the light with one hand while holding onto Chucka's with the other.

Chucka flicked the light switch off, spun her around and into his arms as the door closed shut behind them.

"Let me have another taste of those lips?" he asked as he bent toward her, not waiting for the answer as their lips met once again.

She responded by throwing her arms tightly around his neck while simultaneously encircling Chucka's waist with her vice-like-griping legs.

Chucka, supporting her weight, walked to the nearest wall and without breaking their kiss, started a slow, circular grinding motion with his pelvis.

He could feel the heat from between her thighs right through his clothing.

She was on fire, but contained herself enough to stop the impeding orgasm that she felt he was rapidly approaching. She pushed him away gently while saying, "Go make us some drinks, I gotta use the john, remember."

"I take J&B with a splash," Jan called from the bedroom. "I'll only be a moment."

Chucka had already poured two glasses half-filled with of Chivas Regal that was behind the bar in the corner of the living room. "What the hell, she'll never know the difference", he thought. He put an ice cube in each glass and a splash of water in just one. He usually took his scotch straight up but this time he decided to have it with ice. He rationalized that it would cool off his burning lips.

He looked up from behind the bar and began to survey the room. It was expensively and smartly decorated.

"Nice place," He yelled to her in the bedroom. "You have good taste."

"Thanks", she said as she entered the room in a very sexy emerald silk lounging pajamas, "I'm glad you approve."

Looking her up and down, Chucka volunteered, "I sure do!"

Jan accepted the drink Chucka handed her from behind the bar. She raised her glass in toast and exclaimed, "Shlanta!"

"Now, that's one I never heard before. What's it mean?", Chucka quizzed.

"It's Gaelic for good luck and health," she offered.

"I'll drink to that," Chucka replied, gulping the balance of his drink.

"You know," Janice said curiously, "this taste too good to be J&B."

Son-of-a-bitch! she could actually tell the difference in her liquor. He gained sudden respect for this very different gal.

Chucka came around and to the front of the bar where Janice stood. With his hand on her shoulders and holding her close, he looked deep into her dark eyes. For what appeared to be several moments for both of them, but was really about ten seconds, he searched out the depths of them, right down to her very soul. He continued to stare at her. They were by far her best features. They seemed to be bottomless. He reached up with his hand and touched her cheek.

Slowly he leaned forward and kissed her gently on the lips. It wasn't a passionate kiss, but it lasted for several long, pleasant moments. Their lips parted and he took her in his arms once more.

This time the kiss was more passionate. She let his tongue into her mouth and soon was meeting his tongue with hers, demandingly kissing him, pressing him against her.

"Oh, shit, Chucka," She sighed softly. "OH shit, yes, please make love to me."

For a brief moment he embraced her, feeling the magnificent swells of her breasts against his chest. Then, wrapping an arm around her, they went into the bedroom. Standing at the foot of the bed, she looked up at him again. He bent down and kissed her long and hard. This time her tongue eagerly sought out his and engaged it in the combat of French-kissing.

He held her by the shoulders for a long moment before his hands went to the front of her pajamas, undoing the buttons carefully, one by one. Pushing the material aside, Chucka ran his fingers over the swelling of her breasts at the top, then around and to the bottom, cupping them from underneath, enjoying the feeling of them.

30

He was amazed at the size of them. For such a short girl, her breasts were amazingly large. He felt the bulbous weight fill his palms--full and firm.

He took her nipples between his thumb and forefinger and stimulated them until they grew rigid and hard. Her nipple stood out about a half inch from the areole, and this turned him on immensely.

He then kissed her again, hard, and long.

"I think I can use another drink," Janice said softly after they broke their embrace.

Chucka took the hint and not wanting to press her, went back into the living room and to the bar. He'd leave her alone to undress and get into bed. He decided that a glass of wine would be better for them than more hard liquor.

When he came back into the bedroom with the two goblets of red wine, she was completely naked, in bed and with the sheet pulled up to her neck.

Chucka laughed.

"What's so funny?", Janice demanded.

"I'm sorry," he said, "It's just that I'm not used to modest women."

He handed her the glass of wine and theorized that it must have been the alcohol that made her so brazen in her car.

"I should throw this in your face for that," Janice said with twinkling eyes that gave away her true feelings.

It was obvious to Chucka that she was getting over any reservations that she may have had about being naked in front of a man.

"You're not a virgin, are you?" the thought suddenly occurring to him. It was an alarming thought.

Now it was Janice's turn to laugh. "Of course not, silly"

They put the glasses down and were soon in each other's arms.

Chucka longed to pull the sheet off her at once but decided to wait.

He started to get undressed slowly, Janice watching him with an embarrassed interest.

Soon naked, he climbed into bed beside her, and she came to him immediately. He felt the softness of her body against his and liked it very much.

He drew her to him for a long, passionate kiss. His hand once again sought out her breasts and played in the luxurious fullness of them.

"You can see me if you want, Chucka," she said while sheepishly drawing the sheet away from her body.

Chucka marveled at her large bare breasts at first. They were tipped with large, round, and now erect nipples. They protruded about half an inch and Chucka just loved that. From there, his eyes wandered down and over the slight bulge of her belly to the dark triangle of her Venus mound.

Her hips were wide and smoothe. Her legs were short but well shaped. Her skin was tanned and flawless.

"Two can play this game," Chucka said, throwing the covers off himself.

They both laughed for just a second before drawing their naked bodies together. Chucka started kissing her more passionately.

Slowly his hand ran down her body till it rested on the heavy bush between her thighs. He felt her stiffen slightly, then relax her legs, letting his hand press between them.

"Oh, Chucka," Janice moaned and pressed herself more fully against him.

He kissed her again and his finger found its way into her, moving slowly in and out of her tightness until she was well lubricated.

"I'm ready," Janice moaned against his ear, "Chucka darling, I'm ready for you."

Chucka rolled on top of her, supporting his weight on his elbows and knees.

Janice's arms circled his neck and drew him harder against her. She spread her legs, enabling easier access to her private parts.

Chucka parted the lips of her labia and position himself to bring the head of his penis into contact with the entrance of her vagina.

Janice stiffened for only a brief moment, then raised her legs.

Chucka slipped easily into her now moist interior. His first stroke was gentle and slow. The beautiful sensation of being inside of her fired his sexual desires and increased the speed of his trusting to a piston-like fashion.

Janice was now moaning uncontrollably. She kissed him in sexual frenzy, all about his face and neck while trashing under him.

"Yes, yes, fuck me," she cried, as he pounded the full length of his manhood into her, his glans just touching her cervix with each thrust.

"Oh--you're hurting me. You're too large for me. Oh, uh, ooooh--," she groaned, "ooooh--I'm gonna cum, oh. Harder, yes, please, harder, fuck me harder!"

Chucka thrust faster and faster, trying to get deeper and deeper; trying to hit her cervix when he reached the end of each down-thrust. Faster and faster, harder, and harder. Chucka was now on the verge of his own violent orgasm. He could feel it welling up from deep within. He continued to hit bottom with each stroke.

They came together in such a frenzied orgasm that Chucka thought was never going to end, not that he wanted it to.

"Oh God! Oh God!" Escaped from deep within Janice.

They now lay still, both in each others' arms, breathing heavily, Chucka still inside of her. A veneer of perspiration covered their bodies.

After a long moment, Chucka rolled off of her and reached for his pack of cigarettes in his shirt, which now was lying in a heap on the floor next to the bed. He lit two and handed one to Janice. She silently accepted it.

They sipped their wine and lie facing each other, staring deep into each other's eyes.

CHAPTER EIGHT

C hucka shut off the flame under the coffee. Clad only in his drawers, he poured a cupful. He liked it black. He sipped some and then reached for his pack of Marlboro.

Ever since the wedding last Saturday, he couldn't get the thought out of his mind. Chucka surmised that Jerry didn't want him as a partner since he never called on Monday, and here it was Wednesday and still nothing. Would have been nice though, owning his own business.

Distraught, he mechanically fried himself an egg. He made himself an egg and coffee every day for breakfast, but this morning he couldn't eat. All he wanted was coffee.

The shattering ring of the telephone rocked the silence and shocked his mind back to reality and consciousness.

"Finally!" Chucka thought. "That's got to be Jerry."

"Hello," answering the phone confidently.

"Hi, Chucka, it's me," the girl on the other end of the line said.

Disappointedly, Chucka asked, "And just who is me?"

"Uh, oh--it's worse than I thought. You don't even know your name," the caller kidded.

annoyance in his voice, "I'm in no mood for jokes?"

'It's Sheila, silly," the caller said.

"Oh, Cookie Babe, I'm sorry," he apologized.

"I meant to call you, to find out how you were feeling. I guess I just got caught up in things," he lied.

"How 'ya feelin'?" he asked sincerely.

"Much better, thanks," Sheila answered, "but the doctor wants me to stay in bed another day or so. And that's why I called. I'd like you to do me a favor if you would," she asked sweetly.

"Sure thing, Babe. You know I'd do anything you asked," he said, "What can I do for you?"

"Well, since I can't leave the house," she said sheepishly, "I was wondering if you could pick up some groceries for me. I haven't eaten anything for four days, outside of juices."

"Poor kid, you must be starving," he said, genuinely concerned. "Give me an hour to get dressed and pick up some food and I'll be over, okay?"

"I really appreciate it, Chucka. I don't know how to thank you, you're such a dear," Cookie said.

"Oh, I'll think of something," Chucka said amusingly.

"Tisk, tisk, tisk, --Chucka! You and your mind," she laughed. "I'll see you later, but you'll have to promise to be a good boy."

"Scouts honor," he said and raised three fingers in a boy scout salute. "Bye-bye."

CHAPTER NINE

Although he was sure of how he felt toward Cookie, and indeed thought of her as a very special person, he was afraid to pour out his romantic feelings to her--afraid of being rejected--so he would just say nothing.

Chucka busied himself in preparation to leave. He felt perky now, and no longer depressed with thoughts of a business and Jerry.

Cookie fixed herself a drink and walked nervously about her small apartment. It was her third since she had called Chucka. It was a strong one, this time she had made it a double. She stood by her sofa jiggling the ice around in the glass to get the liquor cooled enough to drink.

It was almost two weeks since she'd spent hours together in lovemaking with Chucka. In those two weeks she had been in a state of intense self-examination and analysis.

As she paced restlessly about her living room, Cookie realized that despite all the questions and the possible solutions she had replayed in her mind in the last two weeks, nothing had been resolved.

She had promised herself, for one, that she wouldn't get involved with Chucka again and not date him anymore. She knew she couldn't avoid him because they worked for the same studio. She had contemplated quitting but decided against it. She had even gone so far as to get her brother, Jerry, to fill in for her last Saturday, feigning illness in order to avoid Chucka.

She was successful in avoiding him. For the past two weeks she attempted to suppress the unfamiliar feelings that were invading her privacy.

She was determined to find out if it was anything more than a physical attraction. That's why she had called him. That's why she feigned sickness last weekend. That's why she hadn't called him in two weeks.

Yet, here she was, a lustful tingling rushing around her groin just thinking about his being there in the next few moments. She had suppressed her desire for Chucka--up till now.

But she didn't want to feel this way. She wanted it to be something more with Chucka--something that went beyond great sex together. Did this great sexual compatibility rule out a deeper relationship? That's what she was determined to find out.

Cookie gulped down her drink just as the bell rang. She froze. she knew it had to be him.

Still clad in pajamas, she quickly lay on the couch where she had previously placed a pillow and blanket, simulating a sickbed.

She took one quick spray of Bianca to hide the smell of alcohol on her breath and in a feigned low voice, called, "Come in. The doors open."

Chucka struggled with the door handle--his hands full with two bags of groceries. He finally entered and went directly to the table where he deposited the parcels. "Whew, made it," he said with painted breath.

He walked over to the sofa where Cookie lies covered with the blanket up to her neck, knelt on one knee, handing her a small bouquet of various colored flowers, and asked, "Men still do this, don't they?"

"Only when they're as nice as you," Cookie replied, stifling a choke that was welling up in her throat. She smiled sweetly, "Thanks, they're lovely."

"I just love it when you smile. It brightens my life." Chucka sincerely volunteered, as he sat on the edge of the couch where she lay.

"Now, --how 'ya doin'?"

"Better already," she cooed.

For one long moment they just studied each other, silently searching for some revealing expression, something, anything that might tip them off to the other feelings, but, alas, there was none to be found.

"It's just like I thought," each told themselves, "It must be me."

Chucka reached for a cigarette, though it was a nervous reaction rather than a desire to smoke.

'Thanks again," Cookie said shyly, "for the flowers and the groceries."

"That's okay, my pleasure, really," he said, "You just lie here while I fix you something to eat. I'm a pretty good cook--know my way around a kitchen blindfolded."

"You shouldn't have anything too heavy," he said, as he took the groceries into the kitchen, "so to start, I'll fix you some egg pastina soup. My mom used to make it for me when I was sick as a kid."

Unseen by Chucka, Cookie was making a face of disgust at the thought of having to eat egg pastina when what she really wanted was a thick juicy steak.

But she couldn't let on that it was all an act--that she was faking being sick.

A short time later, Chucka entered the living room with a tray on which was a bowl of soup, toast, a glass of orange juice, a small rose bud and two cups of coffee--one for himself. He placed it on the coffee table in front of the couch.

Cookie sat up and picked up the rose bud and smelled it, "How sweet," she said.

"At least you have your sense of smell back, "Chucka remarked, "that's usually one of the worst things about being sick."

With spoon in hand, and very apprehensive, began to sip the soup. She braced herself. She was intent on not showing him her dislike.

The soup was quite palatable and, to her surprise, tasted rather good. She smiled, added some grated Parmesan cheese to the soup and silently engaged in devouring the meal, alternating between a sip of soup, a bite of toast and a swallow of juice. She finished with the coffee. Chucka joined her on the couch next to her so he could sip his coffee.

She leaned back and let out a sigh of relief as the hunger pangs began to subside.

"Ah, that feels better," she sighed. "What I could use now is a drink and a cigarette."

Chucka walked over to her bar and proceeded to fix the drinks. "By the way," he remembered, "you were right--about your brother, I mean. He is a good photographer."

"Oh yeah," she replied, "he said you're pretty good too. He had told me that everything went okay when I spoke to him on Monday."

"He tells me," Chucka volunteered, "that he's going into business--processing movies."

He sat next to Cookie and gave her the drink.

"He told you about that?" she asked with surprise in her voice.

Yeah, why? Something wrong?" he asked.

"No. I just thought he was keeping it quiet for a while," she lied, not knowing how much Jerry had told him.

"Tell me about your brother. What kind of...," Chucka was cut off in mid sentence by Cookie pulling him to her and kissing him. It was a mechanical gesture--one designed to change the subject and distract him from his line of questioning. But as soon as she felt his tongue touch hers, flames of desire and lust thundered through her body. Cookie arched her body against his.

"Hey, wait a minute," Chucka protested half-heartedly, "You want me to break my Boy Scout's oath I made to you over the phone?"

"Oh, I'm sorry," Cookie laughed, "I forgot. And besides, you wouldn't want to catch my cold," she said sarcastically.

At least the subject was changed.

"If the germs can take it, so can I," he said, while leaning in to kiss her.

At first his lips gently touched hers and she responded to his exploring tongue as he then took her in his arms and crushed her body against his.

Her tongue came out eagerly to meet his as they continued to kiss. She did not resist when she felt his hands undressing her. She didn't pull away when she felt his hands exploring the roughness of her breasts, or the rigidity of her excited nipples.

When his hand went down between her legs, she let him spread her thighs until she felt his fingers probing past her clitoris and invade her sexuality, now moist and inviting.

She pressed herself to him with sheer abandon and allowed her foggy mind to flow with the building of wild sensations.

His lips traveled to her breasts and sucked the hard nipple of first one and then the other into his teasing mouth. His mouth continued to search downward after the feast of which it had just partaken.

She spread her legs as wide as she could and felt his mouth clamp on her moist mound. At once a surge of sexual sensation pulsed through her body. Her breasts jiggled as she twisted her body under his touch. It reminded Chucka of a fish flailing from side to side trying to rid itself of hook and line.

Don't, Chucka, please don't," she moaned, not knowing why she begged him to stop. Abruptly he stopped, picked her up in his arms, her hugging his neck, and carried her into the bedroom.

He laid her on the bed. She kept her eyes closed tight. Once again, he renewed his tongue ministrations down her perfect body. Again, he found her mound and with his tongue, first circled her clitoris, then dove into her moist awaiting Eden.

She hadn't meant to get this excited, but his expert oral technique was driving her out of her mind with pleasure and joy--to that point where pleasure and pain appear to merge and almost become one.

"Stop it," she cried, while hugging his head to her crotch as she did, thus denying her very words and urging him on in his explorations.

"Suck me," she moaned, "Suck me--suck my cunt!"

Cookie could hardly recognize it was her own voice. Her own words. It was hoarse with pure lust. She liked to talk dirty while making love.

His tongue thrust once more into her. The flashes of mini orgasms blinded her, building to an even greater inevitable crescendo.

"What's happening to me," her mind demanded, "Why am I acting like this?"

Cookie was feeling pleasures at heights never reached before. She hadn't meant to get this excited, but now that she had, she didn't want it to ever stop--not that she could have if she wanted to.

Chucka took the tiny nib between his lips and sucked really hard this time, while flicking his tongue over its tip in rapid movements.

Cookie involuntarily arched her back, forcing her pelvic area even closer to him.

A guttural sound, that began deep in the back of her throat and evolved to a loud shriek as it escaped her mouth, coincided with the release of built-up tension that was now escaping and draining from her body as wave after wave of flashes and colors bore witness to the most violent orgasm she had ever experienced in her lifetime. Chucka was still dressed as he lay with his face at her mound.

Cookie reached out for him and pressed her hand over the bulge beneath his jeans. She first started frantically working at his belt buckle then at the fastening and zipper of his pants. She pulled them down to his hips until the object of her desire was in full view and within easy access.

She grasped his naked manhood immediately and felt the harness of it, the bulbous tip throbbing as she started to stroke him.

She bent her head to it, her tongue licked out and over the moist glans of it. She then tasted the maleness of it and a thrill shot through her body. Her fingers ran up and down the giant shaft that protruded from Chucka's groin. Up and down, up and down in smooth, even strokes. She then pressed her lips to the tip of his penis in a lustful kiss before taking the head of it into her wanton mouth.

With her hands on his buttocks, she pressed Chucka forward so that she engulfed him, his manhood touching the back of her throat and running along the membraned roughness of her thick tongue. She created a vacuum sucking action within her mouth and ran her lips back and forth over the shaft as she guided him in and out.

She nipped along the underside of thickening cock with her teeth, before taking its full length back into her mouth.

Kicking off his jeans, Chucka rolled into a 69 position and once again devoured her vagina.

She could feel the pressure of his tongue deep within her increase as she continued to take him to the root.

She wrapped her legs around his head and went down on him faster and harder, taking the full length of him with each stroke and massaging his testicles with her free hand.

Down below, Chucka's mouth was working frantically on her. His tongue whirled around her clit before jamming it into her again and again as if it were a penis.

Cookie could feel the muscles of her vagina contracting around his tongue. She could feel the first rise of flooding orgasm start deep within her being and start bursting through her trembling body.

As she felt the felt the first contractions of her own orgasm, her mouth wildly sucked and pulled at Chucka's large manhood until at last, in three, frantic, hard strokes, he pumped his hot seed deep into her mouth and throat.

Cookie lay naked and exhausted on the bed, a warm flush covering her body. A trickle of perspiration ran down between her breasts. She could feel the pool of liquid cum she emitted with the violent orgasm she had just partaken. There was also a heavy dampness between her legs where the juices of her own body and Chucka's mouth mingled.

Her nipples were still rigid and hard in their dark colored circles as her breasts rose and fell heavily in rhythm with her fast breathing.

Cookie could not remember having felt like this before in her life--the feeling was like a double-edged sword. One side surprising her with untold pleasures; the other side frightening her with feelings of love.

Her body was momentarily satisfied, yet simultaneously eager to respond to the advances of a male organ. This frightened her more.

"The more you fuck, the more you want to fuck," she remembered someone telling her that in the backseat of a car. But that person remained nameless and faceless to her now. She hadn't believed it then, but now, lying here, having just moments ago enjoyed the most fantastic orgasm of her life and still a second, equally as wonderful one while pleasuring Chucka, she feared the statement might very well be a truism.

Chucka returned from the bathroom after cleaning up and handed Cookie a drink and a cigarette, which she gratefully accepted.

"Thank you," she said, making it clear that she was thanking him for more than the drink and cigarette.

Chucka smiled a kind of boyish smile, self-satisfied smile and gave her a kiss on the cheek.

"Rest for a while," he said in a tone that told her that there would be more to come.

Chucka sat on the bed, and she instinctively put her head on his shoulder and placed her left hand on his now flaccid organ.

"Hey Girl, you gotta give me a chance to recover," he laughed. "You're quite a woman--yep, quite a woman."

"Thank you," she replied, her hand still resting on his naked thigh.

With her other hand she brought the drink to her lips and let the liquid trickle down her throat. The alcohol made her feel warm and delicious all over. It dulled the edge off the sudden lust that had raged through her body just seconds before.

Sheila found that all this newly found sexual desire was rather alarming to her. She normally wasn't like this. With other men in her life, she had been more of the receiver than the giver; always calm and demure, somewhat coy and modest, definitely selfish but never, ever the aggressor. She was never the one to initiate sex with men. She had always thought of it as the man's role to start it off and to make the advances. It just wasn't lady-like to do otherwise.

And now she could hardly recognize herself. She had just experienced the first multiple orgasms of her life and was hot and ready for more--pure wonton lust. Even though each orgasm was totally satisfying in itself, she still wasn't satis-fied--she wanted more.

"Whatcha' thinkin' about," Chucka asked, breaking the long silence.

"Oh, nothing in particular," she lied, "just enjoying lying here with you."

"I'm glad," Chucka said. "I didn't think you cared much for me."

"You wanna know something, Chucka?", Cookie asked. shyly, "until now I didn't know how much." She continued after a slight pause,

"Or maybe it's just that I didn't want to admit to myself that I could be... falling in love with you."

"Are you--," Chucka cut himself off before he could finish the question.

"No--don't say anything," he insisted. "Don't ever say it to me unless you really mean it." He bent down and kissed her hard on the mouth. within seconds their tongues were entwined, and Cookie could feel his strong hands on her large breasts. She felt her nipples harden under the palms of his hands.

"Oh, Chucka, Darling--I do love you," she moaned under his touch. "I do love you."

"I love you too. I have for so very long," Chucka confessed.

"Chucka, make love to me--love me now," Cookie sobbed, half in tears.

She could feel the full lengths of their bodies come into naked contact. She could feel the pressure of his once more erect penis against the public triangle of her mound.

Her breathing started to quicken. Her tongue searched his as her body rose automatically to accept him.

"Fuck me," Cookie panted, "I want you in me--in me hard."

She was on her back now. Her legs spread wide as Chucka maneuvered himself between her thighs.

Cookie felt the pressure of his maleness on the entrance to her waiting vagina for the first time. She raised her legs and felt his rather large penis slip past the pouting lips at her entrance, rubbing all the while against her bloated clit, and ever so slowly fill her exquisitely to capacity. He gained complete entrance with his first slow thrust. She had never been filled quite so completely. She savored the luxuriousness of the feeling.

She cried out with pleasure, "Oh, ah--please, yes-- do it to me hard." Cookie clutched him to her, feeling the muscles of his body against the softness of her own. Feeling the thrusting shaft of her lover deep inside the walls of her vagina.

Almost immediately Cookie felt herself approaching a climax. It burst through her body, bringing perspiration out to make her skin shiny.

"Oh--ooh--ah-ahgahgggggggg!! Oh! Don't stop! Keep going--just a little--ooooh--------fuck!" And Cookie came with a violence she had not experienced before.

CHAPTER TEN

"Caesar, you're my consigliere but more than that you are my friend. As my friend you're your Godfather, I'm giving this to you. I want you to handle this personally because it affects you too and our thing. We don't want Joe Jr. anywhere near this, for obvious reasons. I wanted to start the ball rolling and put a hefty bounty on the head of the person who gave the order to shoot Chucka and tried to take me out. It goes without saying but I'll say it anyway. The old man who sanctioned the hit.", confided Joe Columbo.

Caesar pondered in his own mind whom he should give the contract to. He didn't have to think long. There was no one better than their number one best button...and that would be Chucka himself. How ironic it would be that Chucka would now get paid for settling up with the man who hired this black guy, named Johnson, who tried in vain to kill him and Joe.

That had to be crazy Joe Gallo. This hit also would have to have been sanctioned by the boss, old man Carlo Gambino; boss of all bosses of the five New York City crime families...

After his release from the hospital, Chucka was summoned to Caesar's home.

"OK, we've been friends too long for you to bull-shit me now. You *'summoned'* me, so it must be serious. Your consigliere, what'd I do wrong now?" Chucka said, half-heartedly.

"It's nothing like that", Caesar chuckled. "I think your gonna' like this.", Caesar slides a folder across the table and tells Chucka, as he got more serious, "Here is the important data on two designated targets."

Chucka opens it and reveals the photo of Crazy Joe Gallo and Carlo Gambino.

"I want you to handle this personally. We don't want Joe junior anywhere near this.", he said.

Caesar leans in and says in a low determined voice, "Joe's taking a gamble, a shot to head the commission. He doesn't want to go charging in, fifty guys with guns blasting. Too much chance for collateral damage. We want a surgical strike. Make it look like a natural or accidental death. Don't want anybody linking it back to us. So as little of this will hit the papers as possible. No sense in getting the public all riled-up over this. It will be better for the commission and our future position on it." Caesar picks up a duffel bag and hands it to Chucka.

"Wow bello...How much is here? Looks like a lot.", Chucka choked.

"One Million. It's the biggest fee anyone ever got for two contracts." Caesar exclaims. "The fee is special because of the designated targets."

Caesar and Phil get up and walk toward the door. They give each other the Italian hug and kiss on the cheek.

"I'll leave it to your expertise as to how", Caesar exclaimed.

He opened his front door and Chucka exited with the duffel bag in one hand and his car keys in the other.

CHAPTER ELEVEN

C hucka lay back on his bed, eyes fixed on the ceiling tiles while his mind viewed various ways of assassination. A bomb has too much chance of collateral damage. An up-close shooting would definitely not secure a successful get-away. He would have to think about this some more.

"On March 23, 1994, the medical examiner viewed the body of Ronald Opus and concluded that he died from a shotgun wound to the head. Mr. Opus had jumped from the top of a ten-story building intending to commit suicide. He left a note to the effect indicating his despondency. As he fell past the ninth floor his life was interrupted by a shotgun blast passing through a window, which killed him instantly. Neither the shooter nor the deceased was aware that a safety net had been installed just below the eighth-floor level to protect some building workers and that Ronald Opus would not have been able to complete his suicide the way he had planned."

"Ordinarily," Dr Mills continued, "A person, who sets out to commit suicide and ultimately succeeds, even though the mechanism might not be what he intended, is still defined as committing suicide." That Mr. Opus was shot on the way to certain death, but probably would not have been successful because of the safety net, caused the medical examiner to feel that he had a homicide on his hands.

The room on the ninth floor, where the shotgun blast emanated, was occupied by an elderly man and his wife. They were arguing vigorously, and he was threatening her with a shotgun. The man was so upset that when he pulled the trigger, he completely missed his wife, and the pellets went through the window striking Mr. Opus. When one intends to kill subject "A" but kills subject "B" in the attempt, one is guilty of the murder of subject "B".

When confronted with the murder charge the old man and his wife were both adamant and both said that they thought the shotgun was unloaded. The old man said it was a long-standing habit to threaten his wife with the unloaded shotgun. He had no intention of murdering her. Therefore, the killing of Mr. Opus appeared to be an accident; that is, if the gun had been accidentally loaded. The continuing investigation turned up a witness who saw the old couple's son loading the shotgun about six weeks prior to the fatal accident. It transpired that the old lady had cut off her son's financial support and the son, knowing the propensity of his father to use the shotgun threateningly, loaded the gun with the expectation that his father would shoot his mother. Since the loader of the gun was aware of this, he was guilty of the murder even though he didn't actually pull the trigger. The case now becomes one of murder on the part of the son for the death of Ronald Opus.

Now comes the exquisite twist.

Further investigation revealed that the son was, in fact, Ronald Opus. He had become increasingly despondent over the failure of his attempt to engineer his mother's murder. This led him to jump off the ten-story building on March 23rd, only to be killed by a shotgun blast passing through the ninth story window. The son had actually murdered himself, so the medical examiner closed the case as suicide."

"Too complicated and too many unknowns with too many ifs and maybes", Chucka thought. He keeps thinking about the recent attacks by foreign counties and their assassinations. Iran, China, Russia, and North Korea are some of the countries that come to mind. Poison was their choice of conduit to murder. But how it is delivered is the trick to it all.

CHAPTER TWELVE

C hucka starts the research which may enable him to come to a final decision. He enters the library on fifth avenue, the one with the two entrance lion statues. He goes inside and directly to the card lookup section. There he looks up assassinations and how they are delivered. He retrieves the five books and takes a seat at the far table, the one with one other reader.

At first glance she looked to be young, about twenty. Petite but with a full rack, they made eye contact, which produced a coy smile from each other.

Chucka started reading but had a hard time concentrating. His train of thought kept being interrupted. He caught her taking glimpses of him from time to time and again smiled. She then started to write but stopped and said, "Oh shit! The pen went dry."

Looking up and into Chucka's eyes she asked, "Do you have an extra pen I can borrow?"

Not yet needing to use the only pen he had on him, Chucka offered it saying, "I'm Phil. My friends call me Chucka, non-friends can kiss my ass."

"I'm Colleen. and I think you're being too kind to your non-friends, Phil."

That was an invitation line that he was not going to let slide, so he jumped all over it, saying, "If you don't want to be my friend, I can live with that, as long as you let me reciprocate by letting me kiss your lovely ass."

Colleen flips her head of shoulder length brownish red hair to the side, stands up, walks over, and takes the seat next to Phil. She leans in and takes the pen from his reaching hand. She continues to hold his hand while saying, "Your place or mine?"

A little forward but he liked it, her using the line a guy usually uses and it turned him on. They each checked out their wanted books, while each simultaneously checked out the other.

They were soon outside hailing a cab. Once inside the cab, Phil gave the driver his address and turned to kiss Colleen. She welcomed him with a deep French kiss. No words were spoken and only the occasional sigh was heard. Both of their hands were busy, searching out the various erogenous zones that turned each other on, wanting more.

Phil ran his hands up and down he sides, outside the clothes she was wearing,

Colleen was busy rubbing his manhood, tracing it's length and breadth with a finger, going ever so slowly and then increasingly faster. Phil put his hand over hers and says, "You better stop what you're doing right now before we can't stop."

"I don't want to stop either but not in my new clothes", she retorted.

Both chuckled and straightened themselves while the cabby pulled to the curb at Phil's home.

They stumbled through the front door and immediately embraced. He backed Colleen up and against the foyer wall and grabbed a cheek of her ass in each hand. She raised her legs and surrounded his hips. They rubbed their groins together while Phil cupped the bottom of each breast in his palms.

They enjoyed another kiss before parting with further anticipation. Colleen excuses herself to the ladies' room while Phil relaxes, pours two drinks, and retires the bedroom. He strips to his shorts and lies on the bed.

Colleen enters the room wearing only her bikini under-shorts. She stands and poses for him, then slowly walks toward him. She moves like a stalking cat ready to pounce on her prey.

Phil sits up and accepts Colleen in his arms. They recline in a passionate kiss. Their bodies intertwined and for an instant reminded Phil of the lovebugs on your windshield when in season.

Phil reaches under Colleen's Bikini shorts and slides them down and off of her anxious body. Kissing his way down her body, starting with each nipple and across her stomach while paying special attention to her belly-button region. Then he teased her a bit by playing directly above her mound and now throbbing clit. At this point he dives in with lustful abandon and he now can hear her cries of orgasmic pleasure. He sucks on that clit like it was a miniature penis, bringing her to escape an abandoned, unrestricted, lustful groan deep in her throat.

Colleen at this point cannot control herself, she is so much in heat. She straddles Phil and starts the slow grinding uninhibited sex.

It was a short time later that Phil selfishly cums in a breath-taking orgasm and while still inside her says, "That was just a starter cum... takes all the emergencies out of it and allows me to settle in and bring you to sexual heights you have never reached before."

Colleen smiles and continues without missing a stroke.

Phil changes position and takes Colleen from the rear. Every five minutes he would move into a more erotic position that allowed him to hit her cervix, hitting 'bottom' as they say.

Colleen rolls over in total exhaustion, reaching out to Phil, and just holding his hand. She exhaustedly said in a breathless, panting voice,

"Wow! I thought I died and went to sex heaven!"

OH! how he liked those Irish girls!

~ ~

Results of Chucka's Research

Toxic drugs, snake bites, secret agents:

Assassination is the murder of a prominent or important person, such as a head of state, head of government, politician, world leader, member of a royal family or CEO. The murder of a celebrity, activist, or artist, though they may not have a direct role in matters of the state, may also sometimes be considered an assassination. An assassination may be prompted by political and military motives, Mafia power struggles or it may be done for financial gain, to avenge a grievance, from a desire to acquire fame or notoriety, or because of a military, security, insurgent or secret police group's command to carry out the assassination.

Acts of assassination have been performed since ancient times. A person who carries out an assassination is called an assassin or hitman.

In the case of state-sponsored assassination, poisoning can be more easily denied. Georgi Markov, a dissident from Bulgaria, was assassinated by ricin poisoning. A tiny pellet containing the poison was injected into his leg through a specially designed umbrella. Widespread allegations involving the Bulgarian government and the KGB have not led to any legal results. However, after the fall of the Soviet Union, it was learned that the KGB had developed an umbrella that could inject ricin pellets into a victim, and two former KGB agents who defected stated that the agency assisted in the murder. The CIA made several attempts to assassinate Fidel Castro; many of the schemes involving poisoning his cigars. In the late 1950s, the KGB assassin Bohdan Stashynsky, killed Ukrainian nationalist leaders Lev Rebet and Stepan Bandera with a spray gun that fired a jet of poison gas from a crushed cyanide ampule, making their deaths look like heart attacks. A 2006 case in the UK concerned the assassination of Alexander Litvinenko who was given a lethal dose of radioactive polonium-210, possibly passed to him in aerosol form sprayed directly onto his food.

Assassination is the murder of a prominent or important person, such as a head of state, head of government, politician, world leader, member of a royal family or CEO. The murder of a celebrity, activist, or artist, though they may not have a direct role in matters of the state, may also sometimes be considered an assassination. An assassination may be prompted by political and military motives, or done for financial gain, to avenge a grievance, from a desire to acquire fame or notoriety, or because of a military, security, insurgent or secret police group's command to carry out the assassination. Acts of assassination have been performed since ancient times. A person who carries out an assassination is called an assassin or hitman.

In the case of state-sponsored assassination, poisoning can be more easily denied. Georgi Markov, a dissident from Bulgaria, was assassinated by ricin poisoning. A tiny pellet containing the poison was injected into his leg through a specially designed umbrella. Widespread allegations involving the Bulgarian government and the KGB have not led to any legal results. However, after the fall of the Soviet Union, it was learned that the KGB had developed an umbrella that could inject ricin pellets into a victim, and two former KGB agents who defected stated that the agency assisted in the murder.

The CIA made several attempts to assassinate Fidel Castro; many of the schemes involving poisoning his cigars. In the late 1950s, the KGB assassin Bohdan Stashynsky killed Ukrainian nationalist leaders Lev Rebet and Stepan Bandera with a spray gun that fired a jet of poison gas from a crushed cyanide ampule, making their deaths look like heart attacks. A 2006 case in the UK concerned the assassination of Alexander Litvinenko who was given a lethal dose of radioactive polonium-210, possibly passed to him in aerosol form sprayed directly onto his food.

When people call a targeted killing an "assassination", they are attempting to preclude debate on the merits of the action.

Assassination is widely defined as murder, and is for that reason prohibited in the United States ... U.S. officials may not kill people merely because their policies are seen as detrimental to our interests... But killings in self-defense are no more "assassinations" in international affairs than they are murders when undertaken by our police forces against domestic killers. Targeted killings in self-defense have been authoritatively determined by the federal government to fall outside the assassination prohibition.

Assassination is the murder of a prominent or important person, such as a head of state, head of government, politician, world leader, member of a royal family or CEO. The murder of a celebrity, activist, or artist, though they may not have a direct role in matters of the state, may also sometimes be considered an assassination. An assassination may be prompted by political and military motives, or done for financial gain, to avenge a grievance, from a desire to acquire fame or notoriety, or because of a military, security, insurgent or secret police group's command to carry out the assassination. Acts of assassination have been performed since ancient times. A person who carries out an assassination is called an assassin or hitman.

PLANNING

When the decision to assassinate has been reached, the tactics of the operation must be planned, based upon an estimate of the situation similar to that used in military operations. The preliminary estimate will reveal gaps in information and possibly indicate a need for special equipment which must be procured or constructed. When all necessary data has been collected, an effective tactical plan can be prepared. All planning must be mental; no papers should ever contain evidence of the operation.

In resistance situations, assassination may be used as a counter-reprisal. Since this requires advertising to be effective, the resistance organization must be in a position to warn high officials publicly that their lives will be the price of reprisal action against innocent people. Such a threat is of no value unless it can be carried out, so it may be necessary to plan the assassination of various responsible officers of the oppressive regime and hold such plans in readiness to be used only if provoked by excessive brutality. Such plans must be modified frequently to meet changes in the tactical situation.

TECHNIQUES

The essential point of assassination is the death of the subject. A human being may be killed in many ways, but sureness is often overlooked by those who may be emotionally unstrung by the seriousness of this act they intend to commit. The specific technique employed will depend upon a large number of variables but should be constant in one point: Death must be absolutely certain. The attempt on Hitler's life failed because the conspiracy did not give this matter proper attention.

Techniques may be considered as follows:

1. Manual

It is possible to kill a man with the bare hands. But very few are skillful enough to do it well.

Even a highly trained Judo expert will hesitate to risk killing by hand unless he has absolutely no alternative. However, the simplest local tools are often much the most efficient means of assassination. A hammer, axe, wrench, screwdriver, fire poker, kitchen knife, lamp stand, or anything hard, heavy and handy will suffice. A length of rope or wire or a belt will do if the assassin is strong and agile. All such improvised weapons have the important advantage of availability and apparent innocence. The obviously lethal machine gun failed to kill Trotsky where an item of sporting goods succeeded.

In all safe cases where the assassin may be subject to search, either before or after the act, specialized weapons should not be used. Even in the lost case, the assassin may accidentally be searched before the act and should not carry an incriminating device if any sort of lethal weapon can be improvised at or near the site. If the assassin normally carries weapons because of the nature of his job, it may still be desirable to improvise and implement them at the scene to avoid disclosure of his identity.

2. Accident

For secret assassination, either simple or chase, the contrive**d** accident is the most effective technique. When successfully executed, it causes little excitement and is only casually investigated. The most efficient accident, in simple assassination, is a fall of 75 feet or more onto a hard surface. Elevator shafts, stair wells, unscreened windows and bridges will serve. Bridge falls into water are not reliable. In simple cases a private meeting with the subject may be arranged at a properly cased location. The act may be executed by sudden, vigorous [excised] of the ankles, tipping the subject over the edge. If the assassin immediately sets up an outcry, playing the "horrified witness", no alibi or surreptitious withdrawal is necessary. In chase cases it will usually be necessary to stun or drug the subject before dropping him. Care is required to ensure that no wound or condition not attributable to the fall is discernible after death.

Falls into the sea or swiftly flowing rivers may suffice if the subject cannot swim. It will be more reliable if the assassin can arrange to attempt rescue, as he can thus be sure of the subject's death and at the same time establish a workable alibi.

If the subject's personal habits make it feasible, alcohol may be used [2 words excised] to prepare him for a contrived accident of any kind.

Falls before trains or subway cars are usually effective but require exact timing and can seldom be free from unexpected observation.

Automobile accidents are a less satisfactory means of assassination. If the subject is deliberately run down, very exact timing is necessary, and investigation is likely to be thorough. If the subject's car is tampered with, reliability is very lo w. The subject may be stunned or drugged and then placed in the car, but this is only reliable when the car can be run off a high cliff or into deep water without observation.

Arson can cause accidental death if the subject is drugged and left in a burning building. Reliability is not satisfactory unless the building is isolated and highly combustible.

3. Drugs

In all types of assassination except terroristic, drugs can be very effective. If the assassin is trained as a doctor or nurse and the subject is under medical care, this is an easy and rare method. An overdose of morphine administered as a sedative will cause death without disturbance and is difficult to detect. The size of the dose will depend upon whether the subject has been using narcotics regularly. If not, two grains will suffice.

If the subject drinks heavily, morphine or a similar narcotic can be injected at the passing out stage, and the cause of death will often be held to be acute alcoholism.

Specific poisons, such as arsenic or strychnine, are effective but their possession or procurement is incriminating, and accurate dosage is problematical. Poison was used unsuccessfully in the assassination of Rasputin and Kolohan, though the latter case is more accurately described as a murder."

Sarin is an extremely toxic substance whose sole application is as a nerve agent. Nerve agents are the most toxic and rapidly acting of the known chemical warfare agents. As a chemical weapon, it is classified as a weapon of mass destruction by the United Nations according to UN Resolution 687, and its production and stockpiling was outlawed by the Chemical Weapons Convention of 1993. Sarin can be used as a binary chemical weapon, meaning two different substances which are easier and/or safer to store independently, then can be mixed immediately before use to create the desired chemical.

A tiny pellet containing the poison, Ricin, was injected into his leg through a specially designed umbrella. Ricin is a nerve agent that kills but looks like natural causes. Carol decided to deliver it at a distance so everyone would think he had had a heart attack.

CHAPTER THIRTEEN

Chucka was getting a little blurry-eyed and resigned to choosing the right way of completing his mission and completing the contract. He wanted the timing of these two hits to be simultaneous. It would send a message only to those who can read the connection. It would also not bring the heat down upon their heads.

So, to do this with precision he needed help. He would call upon a fellow cohort to complete one hit. Only one person came to mind... Carol. The second best 'hitman' working for the company and the family.

"Carol would work on one half, and I will do the other", Chucka thought.

"Crazy Joe won't every suspect anything. And his brother won't be upset enough for a retaliatory strike because the lion would already be dead," Chucka mused.

Chucka trusted Carol. They have history, both as assassins and as lovers.

They first met while on a contract plot that they were both included in. But that is another story... for another time.

This was going to be a special hit, not coming in direct contact with either target. It will be planned not to be readily visible as to being an assassination, but will each be done to look to be of natural causes or an accidental cause of death. It will be impossible to trace it back to Chucka, Joe or anyone in our family faction.

"I do what I do efficiently, expediently and without guilt. And I do it better than anyone else!", says Chucka.

His Chrysler Pacifica turned onto the Belt Parkway going toward New York's La Guardia airport. In about an hour he was there. Phil made his way to the arrivals section gangway to the left end of the terminal. In about five minutes the passengers began to exit the plane and make their way to the waiting area.

"I saw her right away; being at the front of the group to file out and figured she must have been in first class, he surmised. She stood out from the rest of the passengers. She was pure perfection", Phil reminisced.

Carol saw me and quickened her pace, aiming directly toward me. We hugged for what seemed like eternity, but it was all so heavenly. She broke the ice, "It's been too long Phil. I missed you." she offered in a cold non-sexual manner. She refused to call him Chucka, only Phil.

"Carol is the only person I trust enough to get the job done." Phil thought. "She is the best 'expediter' I ever saw. I need her If I'm going to complete the contract." She was also one of the best fucks he has ever had.

Together they retrieved her luggage which included one piece that appeared to him to be an unusually elongated shaped hard cased bag.

On the hour's ride back to his place in Brooklyn's Bensonhurst, they talked about the ensuing missions.

CHAPTER FOURTEEN

Boss of all Bosses-Carlo Gambino

E xperts believe that Anastasia's underboss Carlo Gambino helped orchestrate the hit to take over the family after Anastasia was assassinated.

Gambino partnered with Meyer Lansky to control gambling interests in Cuba. The family's fortunes grew through 1976, when Gambino appointed his brother-in-law Paul Castellano as boss upon his death. Castellano infuriated upstart capo John Gotti, who orchestrated Castellano's murder in 1985. Gotti's downfall came in 1992, when his underboss Salvatore

"Sammy the Bull" Gravano cooperated with the FBI. Gravano's cooperation brought down Gotti, along with most of the top members of the Gambino family. Beginning in 2015, the family was headed by Frank Cali until his assassination outside his Staten Island home on March 13, 2019.

The Gambino crime family is an Italian-American Mafia crime family and one of the "Five Families" that dominate organized crime activities in New York City, United States, within the nationwide criminal phenomenon known as the American Mafia. The group, which went through five bosses between 1910 and 1957, is named after Carlo Gambino, boss of the family at the time of the McClellan hearings in 1963, when the structure of organized crime first gained public attention. The group's operations extend from New York and the eastern seaboard to California. Its illicit activities include labor and construction racketeering, gambling, loansharking, extortion, money laundering, prostitution, fraud, hijacking, and fencing.

So, Carlo Gambino, boss of all bosses, or capo di tutti i capi, had to go, simply by saying OK. He sanctioned the hit on Joe & Chucka.

Young Carlo Gambino

CHAPTER FIFTEEN

C arol sauntered, walking in a slow, relaxed manner, without hurry or effort with that long luggage bag in tow.
She had rented a room about a half a block away, facing
the front of Carlo Gambino's house on Ocean Parkway, just
two doors south of avenue X. Her intension is to kill him but
shooting him with bullets is out of the question. Joe wants it to
appear as a natural or accidental cause of death. She figured he
was old, and a heart attack wouldn't raise any eyebrows. There
was this very powerful drug, Ricin, a poison, that was injected
into the leg of his target, through a specially designed umbrella.
Which causes death to appear natural and does not show up
in a tox screen. It has been used by nations against traitors or
conspirators.

She had to be very precise in her calculation. Her object is
to produce a projectile, a tiny one, with a Ricin poison tip, that
will disappear upon impact and will only have the impact like
a mosquito bite.

Natives in many African countries hunt large animals with
poison tipped dart projectiles by using a blowgun.

She previously has been successful in projecting dry ice.
It is solid when frozen and can be used as a projectile. It will

melt by the time anyone checks the body. She had to adjust it for this situation: Speed of projectile, wind velocity, direction, movement of subject, melt rate and accuracy.

She had to figure all this while considering the effects of a silencer.

Carol was the best at her game. She made her calculated adjustments and settled down in wait for Don Carlo to appear to her through her front open window. Within hours Carlo Gambino, boss of all bosses will have his fatal 'heart attack'.

Old man Carlo Gambino

CHAPTER SIXTEEN

N ow it was Chucka's turn. He had to put his skills to the test. He decided to make Crazy Joe's death look like an accident, a very violent one.

It was known that Gallo kept a lion as a protector against someone getting too close.

The site where Joe Gallo kept his guns, pet lion, and launched an all-out mob war in 1960s Brooklyn.

Chucka chose different aspects of the research he had done. He decided to try poison and get the lion to ingest spiked meat chunks, go bananas and turn his deadly attention to Gallo. Somehow, he would figure it out. He would make all the arrangements. He would choose the best of the world's poisons, not to kill the lion but effect it's mind so it would be overly aggressive. He also had to time it right so that the cocktail would not take its effect on the lion for about an hour, just when Chucka knew crazy Joe would walk the pet lion. It may sound like a ridiculous plan, but it would appear to be an accident. If it succeeded, it could never be traced back to Columbo or Chucka and the "Commission" would not be the wiser.

The ingredients of his deadly cocktail that Chucka chose, included Cytoxan, Adriamycin, vincristine, prednisone, and Rituxan. Ingestion of a chuck of meat spiked with this cocktail will cause the lion to go wild and lash out and attack Gallo and kill him. He deducted that one of Gallo's henchmen would most likely shoot and kill the lion and that would be that... a tragic 'accident'.

For centuries countries used arsenic to poison their foes, but it would take months for them to die. It is color-less, odor-less, and taste-less but for this hit, Chucka isn't going to wait months. Gallo must die relatively soon in this 'fatal accident'.

The family had a friend, Anthony, 'Tony Tunes', Esposito, who worked in the butcher shop where Crazy Joe's crew buys the meat for the family cooking and food for the lion's meals.

It's a curious story regarding his name of Esposito. It appears that in past Italian history, when a child became an orphan during the big war, they gave him, or her, the name, "Esposito". I personally know of six unrelated people with the surname of Esposito. It is the "Smith" of America. On top of that five were all named Anthony (Tony). The nickname of "Tony Tunes" was earned because he had a constant habit of whistling songs.

Chucka sent a crew member who was acquainted with Tony to his home in an effort to win him over. He owed the family a favor. Joe had gotten Tony Tunes out of a jail rap at his father's request and it was time to pony up.

Tony was caught buying drugs in a sting episode that went south. Joey C paid off the judge hearing Tony's arraignment.

Tony had been instructed not to mix the lion's food order with a regular food meat order. He didn't want any chance of a screw-up.

Tony Tunes was given the cocktail, which already had been mixed and inserted into a special jar. The top was fitted with a wax seal that allowed a needle to penetrate and withdraw the liquid. When he was alone, he filled a large injection needle with the poison cocktail and injected it into the meat chunks as if it were a marinade. He wrapped the meat as he always does and marks the bag, "LION".

Chucka read in his research that the cocktail would take about an hour for its effects to be realized. He knew crazy Joe would walk his lion after each feeding time.

Now all Chucka had to do was sit and wait.

"Think I'll call Sheila and check on the kids", he thought.

CHAPTER SEVENTEEN

Shades of light interrupted his brain waves, his thoughts he was having during a spinal surgery to clean out his A3 – A4 – A5 vertebrae.

"This just had to work," I thought, "I have to regain the use of my legs."

"Count to ten", suggests the anesthesiologist. I don't think I made it past three.

When I awoke in recovery all I could think of was going to see Karen. That thought along with a raging hardon made it very clear as to what I was to do next.

I was clear minded enough to understand what was happening. There were two nurses and they prompted me to take hold of the triangle grip hanging over my head.

"OK now you're going to have to help us get you higher on the bed, so grab the bar and pull yourself up as much as you can", said the shorter, prettier nurse in a very authoritative voice.

As soon as I tried to pull myself up, I felt a terrific pain in my shoulder. I had recently fallen in my house and landed on this shoulder. Only after my numerous complaints, it was x-rayed for broken bones and there were none, but the pain still persisted. It turns out that I tore a muscle in my shoulder and injured my rotator-cup. They only found that out when they gave me an MRI at my insistence. I learned the hard way. I once fell in a doctor's office and again they only checked for broken bones when I got to the hospital emergency room. Three years later I was able to convince a doctor to order an MRI which revealed a severed hamstring muscle, and it was too far gone to repair. I would need a human transplant.

I was admitted to in-house hospital therapy ward for a week before I was allowed to go home. In that week I worked diligently with all the exercise equipment they had. I now have limited use of my arm and shoulder.

The medical community is at its breaking point. They are overworked with not enough good staff with training.

Case in point; I was prescribed a medication as once daily, Ozempic. I took it as prescribed once a day for three weeks until I saw it advertised on TV as a once-a-week medication. I had gotten very sick, throwing up daily for a week. The pharmacist showed me the faxed prescription and it said daily. Although I think the pharmacist should have caught the error, the onus is upon the prescriber. I could have sued but decided not to destroy a young PA's life, even though she made the mistake and it almost cost me my life. I told the doctor in charge of the PA, and he will insure further training. I hope he does, that it just wasn't just rederick, so I would not sue.

My point is in the course of ten years, I have had eight instances where malpractice would apply.

Back to the story, after his release from rehabilitation therapy and was sent home with Sheila picking me up at the rehab center.

"Oh darling, be careful getting into the car," Sheila said with concern.

"This all sucks bigtime. I've been away from my family for a week, now, and the first thing I can think of is getting home and fucking your brains out." Phil volunteered.

With a laugh Sheila said in a low sultry voice, "And I can't wait to suck that big cock of yours, but only after you've made me cum a dozen times."

Sheila started the car and drove sexily home.

Chapter Eighteen

She had to know he was cheating on her. How could she not? He explained the phone calls by women and his late-night stay outs as connected with his work. She knew he was a button, an enforcer for the mob. She did know about Carol being his counterpart cohort, so maybe she wasn't so sure. "Oh FUCk!", she exclaimed. "I'm sure I'm wrong because he keeps me very happy. He fucks the hell out of me so I can't believe he is doing it with someone else too. If he continues being the perfect man, why should I continue with this nonsense?", she pondered for a moment and then not wanting to think about it anymore.

"Think I'll surprise Phil with preparing his favorite supper; Sicilian steak and loaded baked potato.", Sheila thought she would reward him for fucking her so well and, "get him so horny that he'll fuck me into oblivion."

Sheila got busy, scampering around her kitchen like a newlywed.

Taking out her cookbook she quickly turned to the tab labeled,' Sicilian Steak'.

She took out two steaks from the freezer and put them in the microwave for defrosting. Once defrosted, she then dredged the steaks in a combined liquid of egg and half & half. Sheila then breaded the steaks with combined breadcrumbs, crushed garlic, egg, red crushed pepper flakes and salt & pepper to taste.

She followed the cooking & baking instructions and instructions for the loaded potato in the recipe book and prayed for the best.

Phil was pulling into the driveway while Sheila hustled to the front door to meet him with open arms and a long sultry kiss.

Phil was a little put back but very surprised at her attempt at cooking. He thought, "Up until now, the best thing Shiela made was reservations".

She held off her own urges to fuck Phil right then and there, but to sit down and have a sexy dinner together. She had preset the table with added lighted candles.

They consumed their respective platefuls of food with great delight. Sheila's recipe cooking turned out great!

Sheila served herself up as desert while Phil dove in with reckless abandon. Sheila wasn't going to be left out of all the fun, so she turned around without letting Phil let go of her engorged clitoris. She found a waiting meat rod, hard as steel and just waiting for her hot tongue. Sheila deep throated Phil but it was just too long to take him to his root. She backed off slowly while her tongue darted around the head of his cock. Then she went into her boring rhythm of predictable blowjob giving: Lick up one side down the other, back up and deep throat, back up and a swirl around the head of his joint. Sheila would repeat this progression without deviation.

For the next hour they screwed in every position they could think of, switching positions every five minutes.

After their last all-consuming orgasm of bliss, they exhaustingly rolled over to take a breath.

Phil lit two Marlboro cigarettes and handed one to Sheila.

"Sheila, I think we should go away; Take a cruise, fly to Monaco, St. Moritz or anywhere you would like to go", Phil lamented.

"I can't right now. I'm trying to get the kids into summer camp, and I got a million things to do. When the kids are back in school, I'll get mom to watch the kids while we go on a second honeymoon. I always wanted to go the Atlantis Hotel on Paradise Island in the Bahamas.", Sheila countered.

Phil was noticeably upset with her decision. He wanted to be out of the country when the hits went down. He would have to make some adjustments.

CHAPTER NINETEEN

P hil pulled the rented Cadillac into the parking lot of the Atlantis Hotel, which is made up of three previous hotels and now merged into one. I believe the late-night TV host, Phil Donahue, owned one of them.

He let the car valet park it while he and Sheila walked arm in arm to the front desk to check in. They were given two keys to their suite at the docs, where the folks with boats have their room suites.

Once inside, they quickly showered together, got dressed again in very casual wear.

They proceeded to wander around the hotel grounds, taking in everything the place had to offer: a swim out bar, wandering paths, indoor and outdoor dining restaurants., fast food handmade bacon cheeseburgers joints, a human slide into the manmade pond at the bottom, beautiful white sand ocean beachfront., and all the water sports and parachute sporting and submarine excursions you could want.

The casino sported the most extensive Chihuly glass chandeliers exhibited anywhere in the world. It was truly the place where the wealthy and famous go to enjoy themselves.

Together, Phil and Sheila partook of everything they could, even taking gambling excursions to nearby Cable Beach in Nassau, Bahamas. That was the only casino he seemed to have luck. He won $1,000.

Just one time, and never again, did Phil ever achieve the feat of having seven multiple orgasms, during one love making session! It's usually one and done.

The suite at the docks of the Atlantis Hotel, had a separate bedroom sporting a circular bed enveloped by a very fine mosquito net. For some reason that romantic setting, combined with a super sexy woman, some Jack, a joint and the occasional hand-made bacon cheeseburger, were the right combination of ingredients to achieve seven orgasms: for Phil, a phenomenal feat and an all-time ever personal best. And if that sounds like he is bragging… That's because he is!

CHAPTER TWENTY

Phil and Sheila, after rising, showering, and getting dressed, go to breakfast at Grotto La Define', one of the inside dining room restaurants. Phil orders a newspaper, 'The New York Post. before sitting down. He unfolds the newspaper to reveal it's headlines, "Mafia Captain Killed by Pet Lion". Phil smiled and began to read the article.

In two days, Don Carlo would have his fatal heart attack.

~FINIS~

ABOUT THE AUTHOR

D an Diasio III is a multi-published author in various forms; columns, newsletters, books, over 100 copyrighted lyrics and music and, lyricist for two off-Broadway musicals: "Rumplestiltskin" and "The laughing Feather. He is an art painter with 54 examples, an entrepreneur, and a real-life gangster with the Colombo Crime Family. This autobiography is titled, "I led Four Lives- Confessions of a Dead Gangster."

Milton Keynes UK
Ingram Content Group UK Ltd.
UKHW010931050224
437294UK00001B/181

9 781637 844083